Clint Faraday Mysteries
book 25
If the Shroud Fits – Wear It!

Clint is Helping Judi Lum, his attractive next door neighbor, put a play she wrote on the stage. They are having a dress rehearsal where Hanson McReady appears in a shroud. Vinny remarks that the shroud fits his personality and Judi says, "If the shroud fits...."

Then McReady is found dead – wearing that shroud.

Cmmt HD: I thought this was going to be an overdone theme. I kept thinking another victim, regardless of the name! I like this one.

Contents

About the author

CD Moulton has traveled extensively over much of the world both in the music business, where he was a rock guitarist, songwriter and arranger and in an import/export business. He has been everything from a bar owner to auto salvage (junkyard) manager, longshoreman to high steel worker, orchid grower to landscaper, tropical fish farmer to commercial fisherman. He started writing books in 1983 and has published more than 350 books as of January 1, 2023. His most popular books to date are about research with orchids, though much of his science fiction and fantasy work has proven popular. He wrote the CD Grimes, PI series, and the Det. Nick Storie series, Clint Faraday series, and many other works.

He now resides in Gualaca, Chiriqui, Panamá, where he writes books, plays music with friends, does research with orchids and medicinal plants. He has lately become involved in fighting for the rights of the indigenous people, who are among his closest friends, and in fighting the extreme corruption in the courts and police in Panamá.

He offers the free e-book, *Fading Paradise*, that explains what he has been through because of the corruption.

CD is the discoverer of the Chadam Protocol for curing cancer.

Facebook page Ambrosia peruviana for cancer.

Clint Faraday, retired PI from Florida, USA, groaned and complained to Judi Lum, his very attractive next door neighbor, "She couldn't act her way out of a wet paper sack with the bottom torn out! Christ!"

Judi called, "Lena, please don't come out on the stage dancing. This is supposed to be a sad scene, where death is stalking you and your close friends, and you know it. It's symbolic of a group of people dying of terminal cancer. You can't project happiness into it. It destroys the mood."

"We don't know that, at this point!" she replied hotly. "For pity's sake, Judi! I have to have a little freedom to create! I can't be confined like this!"

"You can create whatever you like in a play you write!" Arnold Bates Candles, a once-producer of national commercials in the states, replied dryly. "Judi wrote this, and the mood is somber. I would suggest that Judi try to find someone who doesn't take method acting – if you could call what you're doing acting – to silly extremes. All you're doing is trying to upstage the entire cast. I think I can safely say that I'm not the only person here who's getting damned sick of it!"

"Let's not overreact here," Clint said. "Judi is the director, as well as writer. The director directs. The actors do whatever is within the boundaries of the director's instructions. The instructions are that this is to be a sad scene, so the actors present it as a sad scene. Any further creativity is within the bounds of a sad scene.

"On the other hand, this is the third runthrough of this scene and the third time Lena has created something far outside of those boundaries. I have to agree that, should she be unable to present the scene in the manner that her director directs, she should be replaced.

"Okay. One more time. It's getting late, and we're all tired and getting frayed nerves. Let's do it right, this time."

Lena tossed her head and mumbled something about the star having to have some freedom to create.

"Lena!" Judi snapped. "Since when are you the star? You are playing second lead to Irene, and you're not doing a very good job of it! Get it right this time or I'll find someone who knows some small thing about acting! Got it?"

"Well! I can leave anytime you suggest! It's not like I'm getting paid for this! I don't have to put up with it!"

"Fine! Goodbye! Don't bother to apply for a role in any more of these plays!"

"Well ... I 'm sorry. I just get into a role too deep and guess I am a bit difficult, but I'm too much of a perfectionist, I guess. I'll try to do it the way you want it this time."

Hanson McReady stepped onto the stage from the rear, wearing a shroud, being the one who was to play Death. He said they had to get it right this time. The damned shroud was hot!

They all moved back off the stage and Vinny Bondi said, "He should wear that shroud all the time. It fits his dead personality!"

Judi laughed. "If the shroud fits...."

"Let's get this done!" Clint said. "I'm getting tired of a lot of would-be actors with zero talent screwing up a very simple scene in a play that should be easy to put on the stage."

They did get through the scene without too much more trouble. Judi said it would be fine if they could just do it that well. She couldn't take any-more prima donna no-talent so-called actors. She damned well wasn't writing and directing next year's play!

"I tried to warn you!" Vinny said. "I did it last year, and swore, never again! If it wasn't that this is for the kid's hospital, I'd tell you to stick even having me help at all where the sun don't shine!

Enough already!"

Judi grinned and gave him the finger.

Irene Henley, the real star, came to say she was having serious thoughts about dropping out. If it wasn't so late, she would, but she would never leave Judi in the lurch, that way. Please put a muzzle on that damned never-would-be ham.

The play was about a woman who spent her life working with sick children, dying of cancer. It was a serious role, but she had to project a sense of humor in subtle ways. The timing was being constantly thrown off by Lena.

"She had to wait until now to do this! She didn't do it for the first two weeks, now, with the play a week away, she starts!" Vinny said. "You want to kill the damned bitch!"

"That's the sad thing about life. We have to face the fact death is a natural ending," Lena intoned. Judi could have killed her. The line was, "The sad thing about this life, which we all know must end, is for it to end prematurely, and in such a state as ours."

Death was lurking just to left stage rear, watching from the shadows over a woman lying in a bed with tubes and bandages and three people standing watch. Hanson moved smoothly to the side of the bed as the three watchers seemed not to notice him – except Lena, who threw her hand to her throat and stared wide-eyed at him.

"I'll kill that damned bitch!" Judi hissed.

Hanson touched the person on the bed and the monitor machine buzzed with a straight line showing. Hanson moved silently back and out. The three were staring at the monitor. Lena aping shock to a ridiculous degree. The other two just looked very sad.

"Godspeed, Gail," Janice said sadly. "May you find the peace we are all disallowed in life."

There was a thin black gauze screen in back,

behind the bed, where a shadowgraph showed a woman's figure holding her arms outward, with several small children running to hug her.

"I feel that she has welcomed death – and that she was, somehow, welcomed to a better place," Janice said. The lighting was fading slowly to darkness as Lena's voice said, "We will miss her, but she is better for the way she spent her life! Go with God, my dear, dear friend!"

"I'll *kill* that goddamned bitch!" Judi snarled. "She just ruined the entire theme of the play! I'll *kill* that goddamned bitch!"

"I think you'll have to get to her ass before everyone else in the cast," Vinny snarled. "What a disgusting hammy *bitch*! Three time the play would have said what you were saying beautifully. Three times that fatuous pig ad-libbed it to mediocrity. I'll damned well see she doesn't get a chance to do that to anyone else! Her, excuse the wild exaggeration, career in acting is *over*!"

They came off the stage, the others pointedly avoiding Lena, while giving her disgusted looks.

She didn't seem to notice. "I think that little idea at the end I came up with was just the thing, don't you?" she asked.

"Just the thing to sabotage the play. It was that!" Vinny spat. "You fucking *idiot*! If you were a man, I'd be kicking you stupid ass from here to Centro and back!"

"Why ... whatever is the matter? I just saved a dull ending, I thought!"

"You aren't going to ever get a chance to do that to another writer," Clint promised. "We all intend to see you're never considered for a part walking across the street four blocks away in another one.

"In case we didn't get through to you while we were rehearsing, your attempts to upstage the others weren't *work*-ing!

"I must say your little ad-libs did show a lot about your acting ability. You don't have any."

"That's mean! I should never have agreed to star in this thing!"

Candles was aghast. "Listen, bone brain! You were not the star! You were never the star here! You will never be a star anywhere! Your crap during rehearsal had some of your better lines moved to other players and dropped you from even second lead. Trying to be sexy in the first act of this kind of tragedy was worse than stupid and amateuristic!

"You're through in theater, if I can call this little production theater, after what you did. It was before you, it may be with someone else playing your part. This play was a disaster, thanks one hundred percent to you!"

"Why was she ever in this play, Judi?" Tyna, Clint's wife, asked. "Clint told me for the past two weeks she was nothing but a neurotic ham!"

"I ask myself that fifty times a minute!" Judi replied.

They walked away from her as a group. Hanson came out of the dressing room and said he wished he actually *was* Death out there. That bitch ruined what was a good play with a good solid moral. He would enjoy touching her and watching her die twitching!

They picked up their briefcases and such and went out front, where Lena was railing at her husband and several others, who were telling her she was a ham and an idiot.

"Why are you all being so mean to me?! I mean, I tried to save that silly thing! I should never have let Judi talk me into being the star! No one could have saved that stupid thing!" She saw Judi, Clint and Vinny standing there. "There's Vinny! I had that *teeny* part in his play last year, so I know he's the one who suggested me for the star in this one! He probably thought I could make something of it. He's had a lot of experience in the theater, and knows what he's talking about – which none of those others can say!

"Isn't that right, Vinny? Wasn't that silly play impossible from the start?"

"You were never the star of anything. I didn't recommend you for a part in any play or in anything else. The play was a nicely crafted presentation, with a huge potential that you've as much as destroyed.

"Clint was dead right when you pulled that second bit, showing horror when Death came in and no one was supposed to see him. You aped shock and horror to a degree that would make Theda Bara groan. Clint said it was a pity you weren't on that bed, and that it wasn't for real!"

"Why ... why have you turned on me? What did I ever do to make you...."

"Get in the car, Lena! Now!" Lew, her husband demanded.

"What?!"

"Now! Or I leave you here with your admiring public!"

She started to protest, but Lew had a look that said plainly that she would be lucky if *he* didn't kill her.

"I want to thank you for making this one of the most horrible nights of my life!" Judi called to her, as she got in the car.

Hanson shook his head. "I think Clint, here, should get ready to get Lew off the hook, like he did with those mobsters, when he kills her!"

"I damned well would give it my best try!" Clint

replied. "Let's all go to Gary's and home. I think everyone at the play knew who fucked it up."

Gary was standing there with his young son. He said they could buy the beer and he'd supply the food. "It was a good play, except for a couple of small rough spots. I take it Lena added them on her own?

"It was ending with just the right note, until she said that last couple of lines as the lights faded. I'm no critic, but even with that, it wasn't at all bad."

"It could have been a very good production. It's a good script," Vinny said.

"When she pulled that shocked act when I went to the death bed I was wishing it was, like Clint suggested, for real, and it was her on the bed. She was trying to steal the scene. She ruined it."

"It was effective, except for that. It added to the shadowgraph at the end to have established the unseen presences," Vinny said. "She diluted the effect with that act and ruined it altogether with that little soliloquy. As Judi said, it tossed the whole theme into the garbage bin."

"I think it went fairly well," Hanson said. "The audience didn't expect Broadway, and it is a good script. It's crafted for the moves and keeps things separated enough that upstaging doesn't work for anyone, particularly anyone with no trace of talent.

"I had a director once who ... that's in the past. We can leave our personal Greek tragedies back then.

"Gary, Johnny Partridge said he talked to you about that lot near the cemetery? The one he would like to build the units on?"

The subject was changed. It turned into, if not good, a reasonable night. Clint and Tyna went home at one o'clock. Tyna was only now getting used to being around Clint's gringo friends. She was a beautiful Ngobe who was raised on Isla Popa.

Clint was going to Changuinola before dawn in the morning to help some people who were caught in a land fraud scheme. He promised Tyna she wouldn't be involved in this mess any further than right then.

Clint had just finished his declaration in the court when he got a call. He wouldn't answer it in the courtroom, but saw it was from Sergio Sanchez, head of the police in Bocas Town. It might be connected to this, so he stepped outside and called back.

"Clint? You were with Hanson McReady last night at the play? You and Judi left with him to go to Gary's?

"How did he act then?"

"Besides being royally pissed that Lena screwed up his act, regular. He was a bit morose and a bit pessimistic, but he always is. That's why he fit Death so well."

"Was he carrying his costume?"

"Carrying it? The shroud? No. It was in the dressing room. Judi will return it today."

"I really *really* don't think so. We found his body in the cemetery when Raul went to police the area this morning. He was wearing it."

"How?"

"Garrote."

"Outside the shroud?"

"No. Inside."

"I'm in Changuinola. We'll finish here in about an hour and I'll head right back."

He rang off and thought for a minute. This was weird! McReady didn't have any enemies Clint could think of. Who would want to kill him? Why?

It was definitely premeditated. Someone got that shroud and took it with them when they went to kill him. It was supposed to be a warning to someone, in all likelihood.

Hanson McReady? He was a tall skinny middle-aged Irishman who was average popular, despite his pessimism.

This was a more theatrical kind of thing, what with that shroud. McReady had never mentioned being in the theater, though he was a good study, and more than adequate.

He said that bit last night, Clint remembered: "I had a director once...." He was tied up in some way with acting.

This needed checking into.

Clint went back into the waiting courtroom and apologized for leaving, but it was about a murder in Bocas Town. Sergio called for information.

The judge knew Clint worked with the police quite often, so said they would handle this case as quickly as possible. He had made his declaration in their behalf, and his declaration carried a lot more weight than a group of people who had been charged with the same kind of thing several times before.

He finished and headed back to Bocas Town. He had left his boat in Almirante and driven to Changuinola, so he wouldn't have to wait for the bus. He was back and on his way across the bay in less than an hour.

Sergio was waiting at the police dock to take Clint to the scene. McReady was found laying on the lid of a vault. Diana Veras Silva, 1913 – 1981.

"Think the choice of graves figures?" Sergio asked.

"Probably not, but we can't take anything as rote, yet."

"That shroud has something to do with this, I just know it!" Esteban, one of Sergio's assistants said. "It tells us something."

"It might be there to tell someone else something," Clint said. "We'll have to check McReady completely. There's something in his past. There damned well isn't anything here!"

"I think it's a warning to someone," Sergio stated. "That's the one kind of thing that explains why someone killed him while he was wearing it. It symbolizes something."

"I don't think he was wearing it when he was killed," Clint answered. "The garrote was inside. He either didn't have the hood up or it was put on him after he was killed."

"Doc says he can't tell, because a shroud just slips on and anything not right would look like something that happened if he was slid onto that lid," Esteban said.

"He was wearing that pair of brown khaki trousers with the safari shirt last night?" Clint asked.

"Brown khaki pants, no shirt." From Esteban. "And no shoes."

"So he got home ... he will have been killed there. It's only six or seven hundred meters from here," Sergio mused. "The killer is quite large."

"No way," Clint argued. "No one could carry anyone into the cemetery from that far away without being seen."

"He could be carried from the end and into here, or along the beach and into here. The killer would only have to cross the road, and that could be done easily enough after the bars were closed and there was nothing but the night traffic. One car every three or four minutes," Sergio pointed out.

Clint thought for a minute as he walked slowly around the area, then went to the wall at the side and down to the beach. There wasn't much of anything to be seen. He went back along the path from the lower end, noting the mud puddles, at spots. He came back and said, "We need casts of the wheel prints in the puddles along the path."

"We have them," Sergio said. "Bicycle. Not distinctive."

"If he was brought, the grave site is important. If he was killed here, it probably isn't.

"What was used as a garrote?"

"Baling wire." From Esteban. "He had to have been brought. The way he was dressed?"

"That doesn't ... I think we need to go to his apartment. If his shirt's there, he was brought here," Sergio suggested. Esteban brightened.

"What?" Clint asked.

"It was a bright moon in the wee hours this morning," he answered. "I think his shirt will be at the apartment, but his shoes won't be."

"Hmmm. Deeply pissed because of what Lena pulled at the play, couldn't sleep, walked along the beach. He probably slipped on flip-flops to go to the beach, so the shoes might still be in the apartment. If there's no sign of violence there, you're probably right."

"You ever see McReady wearing flip-flops?" Sergio asked. "He even wore those combat boots around his apartment, sometimes!"

"Let's walk along the beach to his apartment complex," Esteban suggested. "Maybe McReady was killed between here and there."

"I think we'll find his boots, and I think he was killed here," Clint said. "We can't mess up footprints up where they'll show – he would have walked in the edge of the water, probably. Shit!"

"He wouldn't come out of the beach barefoot," Sergio said. "Too much glass and garbage."

They went to the wall, Clint going along the path to the west end of the cemetery and Esteban and Sergio going along the beach. Clint found three places from the beach to the path that would be easy to navigate at night, carrying something. He went along the farthest one to the beach and carefully scanned the area from the water's edge to the path, then the next, then the nearest to the place the body was found. He called Sergio back. Esteban was moving along, looking for the boots.

"They came in from the beach, here," Clint said, pointing to the depressions, two sets, in the seaweed that was along there. "He wouldn't worry about glass or that kind of thing here. He was walking."

Sergio carefully inspected the tracks and took pictures from all angles with the digital camera he always carried. He agreed with Clint that it was a strong possibility.

Esteban called "Oye!" from down the beach, so they went to where he found McReady's boots, sitting beside a tree stump, not far from his apartment. It was close to a major place people went to the beach, so nothing of importance would be found there. That didn't mean every least possibility wouldn't be carefully recorded and preserved. Clint had taught them that the scrap of paper or the used tissue could be critical. In a case of a break-in and burglary, six years ago, Clint had a piece of tissue recorded and saved. It turned out to be the clue that solved the case. The DNA on that tissue was from a person who couldn't hope to explain how it got inside that house.

They soon went back to the station and filed

their legal reports. Esteban took all the things they'd collected to the evidence locker, then Clint went home. Judi saw him come in and came over to discuss what they knew, so far. She was the best agent Clint ever knew for getting information. She just needed a direction to go in finding it.

After they discussed that, Clint went to the computer to trace everyone he'd come across in the case. There's one hell of a lot of information on most people on the web. Once it's there, it's there forever.

Clint didn't find much, in one way, and found a lot, in another. He knew Judi very well. He didn't know many of the others nearly so well.

The murder victim, Hanson (no initial) McReady, 54, was born in Garibaldi, Texas, and had moved, along with his father and mother, to Bakersfield, California, when he was ten. They lived there, then moved to Berkeley when he was 18 to allow him to attend UCB, where he got a degree in theater and the arts. He was in some plays, two shorts in movies, and used in a lot of clothing advertizing. He was moderately talented, and could do character parts with believability. He did a lot of work with children's issues, and was big on the rehability scene with teenage drug addicts and many young HIV patients. He had no criminal record. He had moved to Honduras in 2008, stayed on Rotan until 2009, moved to San Jose, Costa Rica, in 2010, then to Panamá in 2012, saying Costa Rica had gotten too violent and prices were out of control. He was liked moderately, though people found his personality to be pessimistic.

Irene Donlevy-Henley, 37, had also done a lot of work with children's issues in California. It was (supposition) where she met Vinny and Arnold. She was an executive secretary who married Gerald Henley in 1994 and divorced him in 1997. One child, a boy, Daniel Oscar Henley. She had moved to Panamá in 2002 and was active in the educational and medical issues for children, specializing in the indigenous population.

Vincent Antonio Bondi, 33, very little. He had done some work with local theater in the San Francisco area. He was a studio keyboard man in two recording studios, and worked with some big names in their personal studios. No criminal record, except for a minor pot possession charge that was dropped on appeal.

Arnold Bates Candles was mid-fifties. He made a great success of an advertizing agency in California, going national in 1986. He handled some of the larger accounts from then until 2008, when he suddenly declared it was an empty and meaningless life, and he wouldn't live that way, anymore. He had been wrong to think money would buy freedom. It bought a prison! He left his wife of twenty six years and a son, 24, and a daughter, 19, when he started traveling. He had worked down from Mexico, staying in one place for only a few months, then moving on. He found

Panamá and decided it was the place for him! He was still rich, but so were a lot of people here. Nobody gave a damn about his money. He could be just another normal Joe. He was liked, though some considered him to be more than a bit pompous. He sometimes used expressions that were popular in the gay community in Los Angeles, but that was supposedly because he was around them so much he picked it up.

Lena Lewis, typical housewife. Nothing on the net, except a couple of short notes on blogs. Her husband, Lewis Carl Lewis, no mention. Clint knew he was a carpenter for more than fifteen years, and had retired on disability from an automobile accident. He had a small corporation here that dealt in wood products and cabinetry.

Those, and everyone else in Bocas Town on the night of the 4th of April, 2012, were his suspects, to date. The "everyone else" crowd is the group in which he suspected his killer would be found.

He did have a point to begin investigation. First step, local gossip and such. The place for that would be The Golden Grill. The regulars there knew about everything there was to know in short order, though the information from a couple of them was "suspect at best." Those were the true gossips. The others noticed new people. There wasn't a hell of a lot more to do, if you weren't a surfer or fisherman or diver.

Jim, who was always dependable in his information, knew McReady very well. He said he was mostly misunderstood. He was the loner type who simply hadn't known how to relate to people on the social contact level. He had experience in several areas that could help people, and was willing to help anyone he could. He was a bit of an actor, better than he would admit, as well as a more than adequate singer, which only a very few people knew. He had done some kind of work with the police in a big drug sting or something. General vice, that kind of thing. He was a bit of an artist with stone. Lapidary stuff.

Lena Lewis was a dingbat with delusions of grandeur. Lew had a lot to put up with, where she was concerned. Lew didn't have a violent bone in his body, but it wouldn't surprise anyone if he went over the edge and killed her, one day.

Irene Henley was a truly good person who had a few rough spots in her life. She was an angel with the Indio kids. She had the perfect part in that play, for sure! Her boy, Danny, was at an age where parents often had problems, thirteen or fourteen. It would be harder for her here than in the states, because the kids that age generally have a lot of experiences that kids in the states don't have until they're seventeen or eighteen, if then. Pre-pubescent kids here knew a lot about sex. Clint sometimes thought any twelve year old street kid knew more than he did! They had few taboos.

Vinny Bondi was a lot of fun. He knew a few thousand jokes and stories. He was around the Hollywood people for some time, and knew things about them, but wasn't the type to use a name.

Arnie Bates, he didn't know too much about. He had been in Panamá for about four months, but was in Panamá City and David until a couple of weeks ago. People in David said he wanted to open an advertizing agency here, but had as much as dropped the idea, because it would be too hard to fight the established bunch, who were locked into the fifties and sixties type of campaigns. He tended to be a little pompous, and was borderline condescending, at times, but was OK.

"What do you know about that Randy Fledger character?" Jim asked.

"Never heard of him."

"He's been in town here for a little more than a week. He was talking to McReady a few times. They didn't seem to much care for each other.

"He's staying at Olas, I think."

"I'll definitely check that one out!"

"Well, I shouldn't say anything, seeing Faraday

won't believe it, coming from me, but I think McReady was hiding from something serious, and it caught up with him here," Tom, who Clint did *not* like (one of the malicious gossip type), said.

"What do you base it on?" Clint asked.

"Well, a strange feeling, mostly. He was always looking over his shoulder and asking if I'd seen such and such a person in such and such a place. Was this or that one here for long? Was that one married? Did he or she own or rent? Was that so-an-so's boat or car, or did they rent? That kind of thing. He seemed suspicious of people, even me!"

With cause! "Example?"

"Well. we were talking about Obama over at the Reef this one time. Some guy comes to look in the dockside door and he sort of managed to drop his napkin and lean over to pick it up until the guy left. Things like that. We would be talking, and he would, all of a sudden, like, ask me about somebody who was passing or something. Like did I know him, or did I know how long he'd been here or where did he come from. Things like that. Was that woman around for long, because she was a looker, and he hadn't seen her before."

"I see. I got the idea he was, not so much hiding as avoiding something."

"That's more or less what I meant. So we finally agree on something!"

Clint grinned. No one else had anything to add. Jim seemed to have covered it pretty well. Clint said he might just manage to drop in at Hotel Olas to see how the restaurant part was doing, nowadays. Their continental breakfasts were almost famous. He left.

He was just past the Gourmet when Judi hailed him from across the road. He went to her and she said there was a man, A Randy Something, who has been asking about McReady.

"He said he worked with him in California, and was sure he'd seen him on the street here, but wasn't close enough to get his attention.

"I was talking to him a few minutes ago. He was shocked that Hanson's dead. He told me there was someone who blamed McReady for breaking up his family or something, but he didn't believe it. McReady was sour on women – but I think maybe something like that is what soured him, personally.

"There was some thuggy mob type looking for someone, but it may or may not have been him. I asked Manny to look into it. Sort of an 'Enter stage left' deal. Randy's the same, in a way. You just wonder who they are and why they're here at a time like this.

"Lena has a bit of a past. It seems she was in Alabama for a while when she ran away from

Lew. Over a month. He said he didn't want her back, but she came back, anyway. You know him. He didn't have the spine to tell her to take a hike.

"I don't know if McReady was in Alabama at the time. Two and two and all that crap. I sort of doubt it. Lena was miles from McReady's type.

"Candles was seen near the theater about two o'clock AM, but he was probably on his way home from Gary's. He lives about three blocks past. There was some kind of scandal once that he was connected to a mob, somehow. That's a part of the business, sometimes.

"Did you learn anything more?"

"A little. I was on my way to talk with Fledger. He was seen arguing with McReady, or something on that order. Tom thinks McReady was hiding from someone."

"Who gives a damn what that stupid asshole idiot thinks? On what portentous drama does he base that?"

"McReady dropped a napkin and he asked about people who were passing in the street and that sort of thing."

"In other words, normal everyday things that take on a deep sinister meaning after the guy's been murdered, so he can look like an inside character?"

"Pretty much my impression."

"Well, we can get together this afternoon and compare notes. I have to run."

She waved, and went on toward downtown. Clint went on toward Olas. He had a few things to check out. Things that didn't seem to fit what he knew, so far. Things that threw the equation a bit off balance.

There was some strange undertone to all this that he couldn't quite describe. Maybe because these were actors and film people, if very minor ones.

Why were they all here at this time?

Clint went on to Olas. He passed El Ultimo Refugio and stopped to chat with Ronaldo, who was restocking and bringing things for the day's menu. He asked if any of the crowd, other than Vinny, who he knew ate there often, had been in much.

"They've all been in. Vinny a lot. The others, maybe once or twice."

"What about that Randy guy. He come in?"

"At Olas? He's here every night about six or so. Doesn't stay long. Maybe two rum and Cokes. He's medium popular with the girls, and he and Vinny got into a joke session one night, about a week ago. They had the whole place roaring. Dave and Rob came in to play and got into it, but they were outclassed in that department. They both stayed a lot later that night."

"There's a new person here who was described as a thuggy type. He come in or just across the street (The VIP)?"

"Thuggy type? I don't know, unless you mean War. Warren Something. He looks like he's as mean a character as you'll ever meet. You very definitely wouldn't want to meet him in a dark alley, to look at. He's really a nice enough guy. I doubt he'd take any shit from anyone, but he doesn't look for it. He tries to avoid it.

"Two big Rasta's from across the street tried to start something with him, just night before last. He seemed to be backing down, for a minute, saw they weren't going to stop, so lifted that Tiger asshole clear off the ground and said, 'You *don't* want to get me pissed! You *really* don't!' and sat him down.

"Guess who couldn't get away from there fast enough? 'It was just in fun, man! We didn't mean anything, man!' Shit! Yellow streaks two miles wide down their backs!"

"Well, it was a woman who said he looks like a thug."

"Oh, he *looks* like one. He isn't."

"Well, I guess I'll move on. See you tonight, maybe." He waved, and went on and around the corner. Maybe he'd best wait until he had more information about Fledger and knew something about Warrren Something.

He went to the station to talk with Esteban. Sergio and Emilio weren't there. It seemed four big blacks from Colón had started a fight out toward the bluffs. Some people were cut up a bit, and those four were going to a cell for ninety days. They would be convinced that Bocas del Toro was not the place they should be.

Clint grinned. "I know Sergio's not going to do anything one millimeter outside the law. How'll he handle it?"

"The law demands the prisoner must be fed a minimum of one cup of rice per day. It doesn't say it has to be cooked. The law has a lot of things like that in it. We can hold them three days before we must take their case to the corregidor, in cases where we have to investigate because of violent acts. Three days of a cup of uncooked rice?

"We tell them that three days is the requirement for a first offense. Second offense, we can keep them in that situation for ten days. They'll get the point. Sergio will caution them that they may be picked up at anytime for investigation if they have a previous conviction against them. Another officer can pick them up as they walk out from the first one."

"Have you come across this War character? New in town?"

"Warren Seldin. He scared the holy living shit out of me, the first time I ever saw him. He said, 'Hello' and wanted to know where Las Brisas was. We talked. I was going down to that end, and walked with him. He's really a nice enough guy, but I couldn't help thinking that some people thought Wild Bill was a nice guy."

Clint chatted a minute more, then headed for his house. He wanted to check the internet for two people and he wanted to ... Judi said Manny was checking on War. He called.

"Hi, Manny. How are the wife and brats?"

"Better than we have any right to be. How's with you, Clint?"

"Good. I've got a case. Judi said she asked you to check up on a thuggy looking man?"

"Yeah. Warren Allen Seldin. Just a regular guy. Father was a football player, in the sixties. Better than average middle linebacker. Mother was a sister of his fellow linebacker in the pros. He's got the size and mean look, but is really a mild-mannered type. He doesn't take shit, past a point, but has never been known to start anything. He's okay, Clint."

"Exit stage right. Thanks, Manny. Ever heard of Randy Fledger? Around California?"

"Judi suggested a look at him. He seems to have been around some of your actors and producers, at times, but there isn't much. His argument with McReady was about some kind of candid picture that McReady took at a party. Randy was with the wrong girl, or something. He showed the picture to the girlfriend, and it caused a bit of a stink.

That's all it was. Not really even serious. Randy was a bit Randy with a lot of girls."

They chatted a few minutes, then Clint rang off and sat to think. He was connecting a few dots, but wasn't at all sure they were the ones that drew the picture.

Cripes! How trite! What was next? Adding up the anecdotes? Fill in the blanks?

He didn't find anything more on the net – so he went fishing for a couple of hours. It would relax him and clear his mind. He didn't necessarily want to catch anything, he just wanted to get away.

Naturally, he hooked a large tuna and, instead of cutting the line, determined to bring it in. He fought it for the better part of an hour, got it alongside to get a few pictures, then unhooked it and let it go. It would have been about three hundred pounds. He didn't want to fool with it.

He went in, exhausted. He laid in his hammock until time to clean up. He would eat dinner at El Ultimo Refugio tonight. He thought of calling Judi, but she had told him she had a date for tonight.

He called Sergio. Nothing new found, there. His Colón prisoners had started getting loud and he told them as soon as they reached public nuisance limits he had the sworn duty to shut them up in whatever way was most effective. He knew a few *very* effective methods! If it required breaking their jaws to silence them, sad, but it was what he had.

They shut up. Clint laughed.

Randy Fledger was sitting at the bar in the Refugio, talking with Edouard Santos, a friend. He called Clint over and introduced him to Randy. Clint took the next stool and ordered mixed mariscos and a Balboa. He chatted with the two for about ten minutes, then Ed said he had a date waiting, so he had to go. Randy nodded, and Clint said to have fun. Use protection. Ed gave him a thumb up.

"I hear you knew the guy who was murdered at the cemetery," Clint said.

"And I heard you're investigating that for the police," Randy shot back, with a grin. "It's okay. I don't have anything to hide. Ask away.

"Oh! The argument I had with him at the park was one that's been going on for awhile. He took a picture of me with a stupid bimbo at a party and showed it to my girlfriend. She dumped me, and I was pissed, more because I wasn't used to being dumped, I was used to doing the dumping.

"It started a sort of thing where I get mad when I see him, and he sneers at me. It's psychological. I don't actually give a holy shit. It started, and we didn't know how to stop it. I didn't expect to see him, here in Panamá, then there he was. It just came out. We laughed about it later, believe it or not.

"I've seen a couple of other people who were around the theater and commercial thing in LA and environs a few years ago. I was at that play where Handy was the death ghost or something. I saw another guy, Vincent Bondi, who worked studio keyboards with a band I sort of was in for a few records that went in the nearest circular file. We stunk, but weren't about to admit it.

"There was another one who looked familiar, but I don't know his name or anything about him.

"I met the pill who thought she could act in Macon, Georgia. The one who thinks she's a star and couldn't read a line if she had two weeks to rehearse it. Lorine was the name she gave, then. She had run away from her husband. I wasn't about to pay her bills, and she couldn't get a job, so she crawled back to him. I don't know if he was idiot enough to let her come within a mile of him again.

"That's my story and I'm sticking with it!"

Clint nodded. "That's about what I learned."

"That? I don't get it. How could you learn anything about a bad would-be singer and commercial actor?"

"You'd be amazed at what you can learn on the web. Google yourself. Yahoo! search yourself. If you've never done it, you're in for a nasty shock.

"You know Arnie Candles?"

"Doesn't ring any bells."

He looked more than a little scared. "What's the matter?" Clint asked.

"Oh, nothing ... which is bullshit! Anyone could do that, couldn't they?"

"Yeah. It's public information that's there and always will be. You can't take anything off the net, effectively, as the governments are learning to their, as the saying goes, dismay."

"Cripes! I ran off from ... could they find where I am now?"

"Not if you didn't do anything that would get your name on the net here, or tell someone on a blog or whatever you were coming here."

"I don't use the net. I don't know what a blog is, really. I tried an e-mail once, and didn't receive anything but ten thousand lottery winnings and that kind of shit, so I said to hell with it.

"I owe a lot of money to some gangster types in Vegas. I don't want them to find me. It's more than ten grand. I was a stupid compulsive gambler, but woke up. They threatened me."

"Ten grand? It's a write-off. They might break your leg or something, but only if it was in Vegas and could be used as an example to others, or something."

"Really? I thought they would kill you over ten grand."

"People who do that tend to get caught about thirty percent of the time. A hundred grand may be worth the risk, ten grand ain't."

They chatted for awhile longer, then Randy left and Clint ate his excellent dinner.

There was something a little false about Randy Fledger. His reactions and expression seemed rehearsed. He would need a bit more of a looking at.

"Well, Judi! Learn anything last night?"

"I don't think so. Only that Lew smacked Lena around a bit. She had a red spot on her face, and claimed he had beaten her half to death. He said he'd slapped her when she wouldn't shut the fuck up about being the star who saved the show. He told her to pack up her shit and get out, that he finally woke up to what she is.

"Sergio let him go on his own recognizance. She was shocked, the same expression she used at the play, and said she wanted a restraining order against him. Sergio told her she could get that through her lawyer when the court opens tomorrow – except it's a holiday, so she'll have to wait until Monday.

"George said she didn't need any restraining order. He never intended to come within a couple thousand miles of her again. She could stay with Sergio for two hours to be safe while he took all his stuff from the apartment.

"She claimed she was going to divorce him and take him for every cent he had. He said it was in the bank, in her name, anyhow. He might demand half of it if she wasn't out of Panamá within forty eight hours.

"Yveth was the secretary, and told me about it. He went outside and told Sergio to let her clean out the bank account if she left. If she didn't, sequester the account, so she couldn't take anything out without his and the court's permission. The rent was due next week.

"Serg asked how he would get by. He said he still holds the corporation with its own account that she couldn't touch, no matter what. There were no children, so she was getting more than the court would give her, here, and the courts in the states could stick it. He's lived here for more than nine years, and they can't touch anything after two.

"Lew said she should have died instead of McReady. It would solve a lot of problems for a lot of people. He couldn't believe how stupid he'd been to ever have let her come back when she ran away, once. He said he really had trouble controlling himself when he slapped her. It felt so good, he couldn't believe it!

"Anyhow, that's about all to date, except Tom has been spreading some stories. He seems to think you agree with his assessment, as he puts it, of the murder. He's sure it was some hired thing, which means looking at who else was here. His number one candidate is that mean-looking violence freak who's running around town. He heard that guy beat holy living hell out of four big blacks from Colón and told them he would kill them if they did anything to piss him off. That's what he did for a living!

"Clint, how much have you checked up on him? Manny says he's a good person who wouldn't swat a fly!"

"He is, from what I've learned. Tiger and his buddy tried to intimidate him in front of the VIP. He picked Tiger up like he was a little kid and told him it wouldn't be a good idea to piss him off. That's *all*. Tiger and his buddy as much as ran from him.

"I guess I'll have to handle Tom. Sooner or later, I'm going to be forced to smack the stupid obsequious bastard in the chops!"

"Let's see if I'm correct in what I'll tell people. You're laying for Tom, and will beat him to death if you can catch him out alone anywhere, on general principles?"

Clint gave her the finger.

He went back inside to lay on his hammock on the deck and think about this mess as he had his third and fourth cups of coffee for the day. He wondered if Lew had used those words Judi related exactly: "She should have died *instead of McReady*." That particular phrasing could have a very sinister meaning, as well as no meaning at all. He could picture Lew saying that innocently. Almost.

He was going to have to dig a lot deeper into this one if he was to have any answers. Either they were all telling the whole truth or several were lying. He didn't see where only the killer could be lying.

About what? Too much was unasked. They could all be telling the truth, just not about things not asked about.

Another possibility: McReady had been into blackmail. Someone was here to put an end to it in a place where whatever it was about wouldn't ever show up. He did have that candid photo of Fledger. There was no evidence McReady had used it as blackmail. After all, he showed it to the girlfriend without ... what other photos did he have, and what did they show? Could it be that he took photos of the wrong person at the wrong place at the wrong time, that he never intended to use it as blackmail proof or anything else, but the person or persons in the photo had to stop even the possibility?

What about the bit where he did something that caused a family to break up? What was that item about?

He needed more information.

What? He was into understatement again?

He got up and went back to the computer. He suddenly had a nagging suspicion because of something he'd noted in passing. Maybe he'd finally found a connection of sorts, if a tenuous one. He had two little points to connect.

Three. Maybe his data was finally falling into place.

Four! This was getting closer!

Okay. Fledger, Randolph Johns. #6. Born in Brandon, Texas. Raised in Colorado and Oregon until he was barely seventeen, then went to San Francisco. He was handsome and sexy enough that he lived as a gigolo and hustler for awhile, two years, and went down to LA with a John who owned a business that made commercials. He was used in commercials that featured tight clothes and come-on expressions. He became a bit of a ho-hum rock singer, then did two small walk-on parts in B-pictures that were more toward C. Semi-X things. He dropped the hustler part and concentrated on the gigolo acts, then made enough to become independent and drop the gigolo part. He moved to Las Vegas two years ago, where he did a few appearances in the X-clubs as strictly tease. He got into blackjack and lost his ass. He came to Panamá.

That said a lot and very little. Clint thought he

may well be a generally good person who had experienced the seamier part of life and come through in good condition, for the most part.

Okay. He'd seemed open enough when Clint talked with him last night. He was staying at Olas, so Clint went there to find him sitting at a table on the deck, having the continental breakfast. He went to ask if he could sit and talk.

"Ah! The parts we didn't cover last night? You found things on the internet?

"I asked Douglas to show me how to do that Google thing. He brought me up on it. You were damned well on the button with saying I would be shocked!

"Ask away. I won't lie, even about the parts I'm not in the least proud of."

"Well, just from the net I learned you ran away from home at seventeen and lived as a male prostitute for a few years in the San Francisco area?"

"Yes. I had a couple hundred dollars from selling my bicycle and some records and such. I couldn't believe what it cost to live in the San Francisco area, so was out of money in a week. A guy I met, next door in the rooming house, was gay. He said that I could live with him, strings attached, but not too tightly. He said I could make a fortune hustling the gay bars.

"I didn't take him up on it – then. There was an older woman, maybe thirty eight or nine, living downstairs. She managed the place. She made an arrangement where I didn't pay rent and could eat breakfast and lunch with her. It wasn't too bad, but I still didn't have a dime to my name, so I took Robbie up on his offer for cash, for so long as Edith didn't find out about it.

"The sex wasn't bad. It was no worse than Edith, who reminded me of my Aunt Selma. Robbie was a really nice person, and was into one-way sex, which is the only way I would have it with a guy, anyhow.

"Long story short, I soon went to the bars and made a hell of a lot of money. I've always been oversexed, which was part of why I ran away. My father was a lot too strict, and mother was very religious. When they found I was experimenting with Sandra and Emily ... with two girls my age, they went ape and grounded me for the rest of my life.

"Anyhow, that was it for San Francisco. I was for rent to anyone who would go along with the things I wouldn't do, male, female, or indifferent. I was always surprised at how many people are bisexual. A lot of people here are.

"Anyhow, I met a guy who made commercials for sexy men's clothes. He was gay, and said I had a way of looking at the camera like I was saying, 'Want me? Come on! Let's romp!' That's what the clothes were designed to say, so it would be what he called synergic. I made my first one with button jeans with the top two buttons undone, looking at the camera with a raised eyebrow and grin. I have to admit that it was good, and it was damned sexy. I suddenly had a big fan club and offers into the thousands for a night with someone.

"Anyhow, he was in a bar in SF. His business was in Hollywood. I would be mixing with the stars! A couple of them made ads for him for side money. I would fit right in, because I was sexier than most of them. He might even get me in the flicks.

"So I said, 'What the hell? Why not!' and was in Hollywood next day with five hundred bucks in my pocket and a fantastic apartment. I made that commercial the day after that, and was on my way.

"I did the music bit, a little, and went to work part time in a studio. I met Handy McReady there, and we became friends. He didn't approve of the way I made my living, but also agreed it started from desperation and being too young and naive to be out on my own. It was okay for me, but he wanted no part of it. It shocked him when I said

I'd just as soon be with a gay as with a woman, because it was more honest. He said he could tell me stories about cheating, lying women, but never got into it very far. I took it some women really worked him over a time or two.

"He was a bit curious about what a guy would do with me, and vice versa. I told him about it. He said he could never even get it up for a guy. It shocked him even more when I admitted I had done a few things for a few guys I particularly liked.

"It's part of life. I'm not ashamed of it, it's what my life was and it was a life that was good for me, at the time.

"He would take pictures of everything. He had a bunch that were taken at a party. One was with me with my arms around a guy, not with a bimbo, as I told you. My girlfriend at the time saw it, probably because it was in a bunch taken at that party, and was probably not deliberate. Handy wouldn't do anything like that, deliberately. She dumped me because it was a guy.

"Anyhow, things went along pretty well, but it isn't what you'd call a full life, by any standard. There's always something missing, and you don't have a clue as to what it is.

"I got an offer to go to Atlanta for a shoot. I met Lorine there, and that lasted for a week or so, but she was a hell of a pill after a few days, and was about a third as good as she thought she was in bed. She got possessive, fast, so I told her to hike.

"I went back to LA, then got an offer in Las Vegas to do some work at the casinos. I ended up in an X-club, doing a strip for a ninety percent gay crowd. I'd already decided it was purely stupid to continue that. AIDS is scary, and it was pure luck I never got it.

"I won a jackpot in a small casino. More than six thousand dollars. I got hooked and changed to blackjack, where I got into deep trouble. You've heard the rest."

Clint nodded. That was clear and honest. Randy Fledger was out of it.

Clint walked back toward town, thinking. He had to talk with War, then he had to put some things together.

He met Warren Allen Seldin. It didn't take him ten minutes to eliminate him as a suspect in anything. He was really a more than nice person. He was scary, until you talked with him for a minute, then you had to like him. If he killed anyone, he would simply break them in half and throw the bloody pieces in opposite directions. He wouldn't use a garotte! If he pulled a wire tight around a neck it would sever the head!

Clint was strolling past Chitres and Lew was sitting there with Judi. She waved, and he joined them for a delicious typical lunch.

"I was just telling Judi how I finally got the guts to smack Lena in the kisser. I should have done it ten years ago and we wouldn't even be here. _She_ wouldn't, anyway. Judi says she's going to have a special medal made for me for dumping her!"

"As he would say when she was starring in a Shakespearian drama, 'Out, damned spot!'" Judi said, smirking. "Lew says she's already booked a flight to Houston, Texas, where she's going to file for divorce and take him to the cleaners."

"I didn't mention that we have to live in Texas ninety days before we can file for divorce there," Lew said, matching Judi's smirk. "She'll have left the country here, so can't file for divorce here, either. She can live solo in Texas for three months, then file for abandonment, if I'm not there, but she's the one who left. Bummer!"

"Well, life goes on," Judi said. "Did you talk with Fledger? War?

"I met War. He's actually a very nice person."

"Yeah. Fledger is more honest than I am about some things. He's out as a suspect, unless he's one hell of an actor – which his short stint in Hollywood proved he's not.

"War is a very nice person. He was never really in it. Which reminds me."

"Tom?"

"Uh-huh."

"Figured how you'll handle that?"

"Uh-huh."

They chatted awhile longer, then Clint went on. The regular bunch was at the Golden Grill. Clint felt evil, so he went to their table to say hello and talk a minute. He said he was heading on home to put some things together.

"Oh! I meant to tell you!" he said, innocently.

"Tom, it's best you don't be anywhere close to Warren. Several people have told him about what you claimed about him. He said that not much pissed him off, but that did.

"I talked with him quite a bit, and checked on him. He's a lot cleaner than anyone here. He's a very nice, pleasant, even-tempered person, but he does have a line – that you've crossed, and then some.

"I was talking with Judi and Lew. Judi pointed out the obvious about him. If he used a garrote, which he wouldn't, it would have taken Hanson's head off! He's more the type who would just tear a person in half and throw the bloody parts in opposite directions.

"Well, got to run!" He left with Tom looking very much like he was going to faint. Jim was working hard not to laugh out loud.

Damned ass! Clint hoped he'd die right there of heart failure.

Next would be Vinny. Clint didn't expect much, but he would use it to check on something else. He was in the park, playing a game with the street kids. Clint joined them for a few minutes. The kids had all run to hug him when he came up. The kids soon left to sell their tourist trinkets, and Clint sat with Vinny.

"What?" Vinny asked. "It's obvious you have

something to say to me."

"I want answers to a few questions that you may not care to answer. They're from reading between the lines."

"I think I see where this is heading. There's nothing between the lines, Clint. Ask away. I'll answer, even if you ask something too personal for an answer, in which case I'll answer by saying it's none of your business."

"Okay. Bluntly. What was your former contact with Lena Lewis? She seemed to know a lot about your experience with the theater."

"I saw her once in LA. She was trying out for a part in a play where she would be discovered by Hollywood and would soar to soon become the century's top superstar. She got a bit part and screwed it up so bad we wrote most of it out of the script."

"Candles was directing?"

"Producing. That was his first and only contact with her. He describes her as the century's top stage bitch. He agreed with me about not letting her into the play. She can be oh-so sweet and reasonable until she has a part. That's her only real show of acting ability.

"I hear Lew gave her the heave-ho. Maybe he'll be someone I can respect now.

"Oh! No one told you we had met her ... except

Arnie. He made no bones about it."

"Had McReady met her before, that you know of?"

"Only when she was to appear in a commercial for some detergent and ad-libbed herself out of consideration. He didn't realize it until that first time she did the wide-eyed shock act in the play. It was exactly what she had pulled in the ad. Shock and a hand to her throat. Stolen directly from Theda Bara, who was a terrible ham, but an amateur compared to the lovely Lena. Wide-eyed shock at how horrible a competing product was. Detergent, for Christ's sake!"

"You knew Candles, then."

"A couple of ads. I saw a man here who was in some ads there. Randy Something. A really cool sort of guy, but a male prostitute who made no bones about it."

"Then Candles is gay – or bi?"

"No. Not that I know of. Why...?"

"Randy said he went to LA with a gay man who owned an advertising agency. It was how he got into the show business."

"Oh. That was Clarence Biddings Forsythe the fourth or something, not Arnie. He was around a lot, and gave a number of people their first shot at ads. He could choose men everyone thought were sexy. He isn't so bad. He doesn't require too much of his lovers, but it wouldn't matter, if he did. Take the deal or not is their choice.

"I couldn't get into that. What experience I have is not anything that could make me go for the life. It fits some. Randy's a sex addict – or was. Anything goes, but to a certain point.

"What's that about?"

"Trying to find a reason McReady's dead. If someone's a closet queen, that could be behind it."

"Oh. Arnie isn't. He had a wife and grown kids and doesn't go for that. I've heard suggestions from people who take his penchant for being too pompous and critical and some of the expressions he uses as that, but it's definitely not true."

"Know anything about Irene Henley, the one with talent in that group, besides McReady. He definitely had some."

"It's a lark with her. She's into kids, as you can see. She could make it on the stage, but doesn't want the baggage it brings with it.

"She's real, Clint. A minor Mother Theresa."

"That was my impression."

"Help any?"

"It confirms a lot of things I was considering."

"Such as?"

"Sex isn't involved. I wonder if we're being manipulated into thinking it's somehow behind the killing."

"What's the difference?"

"If we're looking for a sex motive, we might miss the real one."

He nodded. He thought of a thing he was considering earlier, so went to his house and onto the computer to research a few things about Los Angeles at a certain point in time.

He was back to looking for a basis of motive. There was nothing in the sex angle, he was now convinced. That was a big distraction that was planted, carefully, almost subliminally. The only purpose he could think of was to hide the real motive. He also considered the professional way that theme was inserted.

He had five dots to connect now. He was sure he knew who, but he didn't have a clue as to why. Without that, he was nowhere.

Damn it! What did that shroud and the cemetery have to do with this mess!? If it was a warning to someone ... it would have to be. There was no other purpose in having those two factors in to add to the clues. It was a puzzle with missing pieces, until he could find them.

Maybe there was another purpose for those two factors! A very major purpose!

Clint considered what he had. If there was a way to confirm any of the first part, he could put the pieces together. The problem all along was one that was caused by expert manipulation. In the language of the theater, the players were being moved from offstage. There was a definite and identifiable pattern.

The first question: Who could have done it.

Answer: most of them, but that didn't eliminate anyone.

Second: What was the motive?

Answer, the missing factor. Clint was sure he could answer that one fairly quickly, now that he wasn't being moved to someone else's direction.

Okay. Stop the procrastination. Get on the net and put that little item in place and it was solved.

He had to put the victim and the killer together before they came to Panamá and discover what had happened in that time frame. That would fairly certainly establish motive, and that's all he needed. The one with motive was the killer.

He had begun to travel in early 2008. The critical period would almost have to be late 2007 to early 2008.

He had come from California, meaning that whatever happened in that five or six months was what he needed.

He checked what he had in his notes, taken from his earlier net search, what Sergio told him, and what interviewing all of them said.

Irene Henley was definitely out of it. She had been in Panamá since 2002.

His first dot to connect, who had been in California in 2007-2008?

Four – well, five, but Randy was only for information. Clint was personally positive he knew who it would be. Randy was *not* in that group. Vinny, Candles, Lena, and Lew.

Someone involved in something that would make them want to kill.

Vinny was out of it. He had checked out in too many ways for it to involve him in anything to do with McReady, in a negative context.

Unless it was a matter of a picture or two, which was probably behind the whole mess.

Candles and the Lewis couple.

If it had been one of the Lewis couple, the other would know about it and would be smashing the other over the head about it.

That left Candles, his choice from nearly the first.

Add it up. Candles had run off from a family at just the time McReady began traveling to get away from something. He seemed to be following McReady. Clint had a factor to work from on what was behind it. If it was as he suspected, he was surprised that Marko hadn't found it in ten seconds. On the other hand, Marko's family was never much involved in Hollywood.

Clint looked at a note and called up the police records files for LA County from June of 2007 to February of 2008. His note said drug sting.

Drug sting with a question mark. "Or something."

Nothing about drug stings and the Hollywood crowd, except for a couple of raids on suppliers and the millions in cash confiscated. During that administration? Clint wondered how much of that confiscated millions in cash ever got where it was supposed to go.

Other things?

Stings conducted in the period involving drugs, auto chopping, liquor, prostitution, art theft, and credit card theft. A major international art theft ring was broken up when an operative found an informer who had seen some of the material in someone's house. In an important executive's house. Some of the art was recovered in other show business people's houses. The executive had made a deal. Some of the evidence against him was shaky, and they couldn't confirm it, but he rolled over and gave them the evidence to convict four biggies. The art in his house had been removed and the supposed evidence that it ever was there was not forthcoming as promised. The informant, known only as "Irish" had quickly disappeared and couldn't be located. It was suspected he had been killed or otherwise silenced.

The executive was never named, but his family had moved from California and was put into WP when he also disappeared. It was later learned he had fled to Mexico to keep from being killed by the other convicted fences.

That fit. McReady was "Irish" and Candles was the un-named executive. McReady had those photos that would prove it was in Candles' house where they were taken, somehow.

Clint sat back to consider for a minute, then got up and went to the station to talk with Sergio. He called Manny (Marko) and asked about that particular sting. Manny said he'd get back. He hadn't checked on anything like that.

"I don't need it, but it would be nice to have," Clint said. "I wonder why Candles kept pursuing this mess when McReady had as much as made it known he was home free for the evidence. He might have even destroyed the pictures or whatever."

"Maybe not!" Esteban cried. "I think there was a key to a locker in Changuinola or somewhere in McReady's apartment. Maybe the pictures are there."

"We can find anything like that fairly quickly, Clint," Sergio said. "Let's postpone anything more until we can check that bit out. Get the key, Esteban. Let's go to Changuinola on a treasure hunt!"

"It still leaves me wondering just why McReady was killed. He certainly wasn't blackmailing anyone, and hadn't acted on the evidence."

"Maybe he was just using the evidence as his personal protection. Protection against his being killed," Sergio suggested.

"But he was killed, so there has to be more than that."

They went to Changuinola in Clint's car. He took them to Almirante in his boat, then drove from there to Changuinola. They went to the main police compound and asked about the key. Capitan Ramirez said it was one of three places where that kind of key was used, all of them private. He went with them. It was in the second place, where an old man and his wife rented the storage bins by the month and half-year. It was paid for another four months. It was a cardboard box with some clothes and a manila envelope inside.

They took it back to the police compound and opened it for inventory, with lots of cameras and witnesses. Sergio signed out the manila envelope for evidence in a criminal case on Isla Colón and they headed back. They studied all the papers and photos at the station in Bocas Town, then Clint said to have the bunch brought in for a Nero Wolfe session at seven.

Then he went home to relax and compose what he was going to do and say tonight, cleaned up, and cooked some shrimp he had in the freezer al ajillo (in garlic butter). Tyna, who was visiting her parents for a few days on Isla Popa, called to say she would be back home in a day or two. She missed him terribly.

He picked up Judi and headed for the station. It was going to be interesting.

Sergio stopped him outside and asked what the part about Tom filing a protection order against Warren was. He answered and told him what had happened. Sergio let a wry grin escape. He didn't like Tom anymore than Clint did. He said he told Tom that, until the man actually accosted him, there was nothing he could do. You can't get a protection order on hearsay evidence.

They went inside. Clint was surprised to see Randy Fledger there. Sergio said he'd never said Fledger was no longer a suspect.

They all sat around. Clint said they were there to clear up a few minor points that should make it possible to close out the case. Most of them looked expectant, Candles looked smug.

Clint began, "This case is about an old revenge motive against a man who uncovered a serious criminal operation."

Candles lost the smug look.

"What happened makes one of you the obvious killer. Your misdirection was a little overdone. Trying to get us focused on a sexual situation was doomed from the very start, though your use of subliminal techniques pointed right at you." He was looking Candles in the eyes. Candles was nervous and darting glances around. "Don't try anything stupid. This is an island and you can't hope to get away.

"So. All we had to do was consider it as a play, carefully scripted and directed by the killer. You are known as a good director.

"To expose that kind of thing means you have to find the non-clues, the misdirections, such as the shroud. That was supposed to make your audience think it had some deep significance and make us look in places there was no information, no data.

"You were seen by the theater after you left us at Gary's.

"We only had one problem, from the first. We knew it had to be you, but we had no motive. If you had done nothing, it would be safe. He didn't use the material in some years. We didn't have a least clue as to where it was, which you depended on. When we traced the keys in his apartment, we found the one to the locker. We have the photos and an explanation."

He took the photos and a sheet of paper from the envelope. Candles put his face in his hands.

"This is the proof we needed for a conviction in court. We had an eighty five percent chance you would have been convicted without it, but we always try for better odds, both because of the court and because we don't want to be wrong where the rest of a person's life is at stake.

"I'll read the pertinent part: I had the photos and Millie was hit by a car that didn't stop. I feel it was Arnold Candles or someone he hired to kill her to make me not produce the enclosed photos or I would have a like accident. I decided to put the screws to him and had a friend I met in the business, a man who played a very convincing heavy, contact Candles and lay it on the line that, should anything happen to me, his family would be forfeit. I then took the enclosed and the money

I had accumulated over some years and began to travel to avoid further confrontation, though I am aware that Candles placed his family in hiding and has been since pursuing me. This is here to insure that, should he actually manage to kill me, he will be convicted in the states for many crimes, his accomplices receiving sentences of from fifteen to twenty five years.

"The fact he pursues me in this manner means he intends to harm or kill me. If it happens within seven years, he will be tried and convicted using this evidence and the statements made at the time of my leaving for my self-protection. I can but hope that, should it go beyond the statutes of limitations, he will also be prosecuted for the murder of Millie Watts, as well as for my own murder.

"The enclosed photos show the stolen articles in places where there can be no doubt it was in his home, as matching the police photographs will prove. There are also the three with Arnold Bates Candles holding three different stolen properties.

"It goes on, but this is all we need.

"Why didn't you just wait? You would have been home free."

"No. He always intended to wait until a couple of months before the statute of limitations came into effect and expose me. He told me that on the little beach across the road from his condo. It didn't leave me much choice."

"So you took the choice of making it happen now instead of in three or four years from now, time in which you could have been out of the reach of the US charges," Sergio said. "I have to arrest you on charges of murder. It's over."

Candles drew a revolver from his pocket and moved to aim it at his head. Esteban, standing close, knocked it out of his hand.

"Have the decency to not make a bloody mess for me to have to clean up," he said. "Let's go!"

Curtain!

Clint laid back in the hammock and watched as Judi and Randy came alongside his deck in Clint's boat. They had taken Vinny to Almirante to catch the David bus. Warren was with him. They were going to try to start a small business. Whatever they decided would make them a small amount to add to what they had.

Tyna brought out a tray of chichas for everybody and went to snuggle up with Clint in the hammock.

"Well, Candles is on his way to California, in handcuffs. Irene is planning next year's play. Randy is planning to stay here for awhile," Judi said. "I think we'll all get along. He fits with this culture a lot better than most, and is decorative!"

"Yeah!" Randy said. "I have enough in cash that I can live very well on the interest here. If I get in bad shape, I can always make a deal with you or Judi to support me!"

Clint and Judi both gave him the finger salute.

Sergio and Esteban came from the front of the house to say, "Judi, the hospital says you were as good as they've ever had directing the play. You

Page 64

are asked to handle it again next year."

That got the salute from all of them.

C. D. Moulton's works are available on most major outlets as printed or e-books. CD writes the CD Grimes, PI mysteries, the Det. Lt. Nick Storie mysteries, the Clint Faraday mysteries, the Flight of the Maita science fiction series, books on orchid culture and many others of many types. Mystery, adventure, intrigue, science fiction, fantasy, paranormal, mild erotica, and factual.